I0746536

FLIGHT TEAM
Graphic Novel

Copyright © 2021 Nicholas Garcia

Printed in the United States of America

ISBN: 978-1-7363069-4-9

Follow

@v1_studios_official

FLIGHT TEAM

Chapter 1

ATLAS PARK HAS BEEN CROWDED EVER SINCE THE CHANCELLOR ANNOUNCED HE WOULD BE TRAVELING HERE

IT HAS ALSO NEVER BEEN MORE DIVIDED

WITH THE RISE OF THE CHANCELLOR WAS ALSO THE RISE OF THE MARTEOUS

ARE YOU SURE THIS IS THE RIGHT TRAIN?

BOOMM

JUMP

VENTUS
EURUS

WOOSHH

WELL
I GUESS
I'M UP

JUMP

SUPERHERO
LANDING!
LOOK FOR
ANY
SURVIVORS

VWOO O O

IS IT SLOWING DOWN?
ATTENTION ATTENTION! HELP IS HERE, PLEASE REMAIN CALM

DID YOU PUT YOUR BACK INTO IT??

WE HAVE HUNDREDS OF PEOPLE AND TO ANSWER YOU MARCOS, THE TRAIN IS INDEED SLOWING

GOOD JOB TODAY TEAM
REST UP, WE HAVE THAT PRESS CONFERENCE SOON
I GOTTA PEE..

I VOWED TO RID THIS COUNTRY OF CRIME
THE PEOPLE OF THIS GREAT CITY HAVE WELCOMED ME WITH SUCH LOVE
AND I AM HERE TO LAUNCH THE FIRST WAVE OF THE PLAN

PRESENT TO YOU...

DEMETRI!!
ON IT

HIT THE FOOT!
BANG!

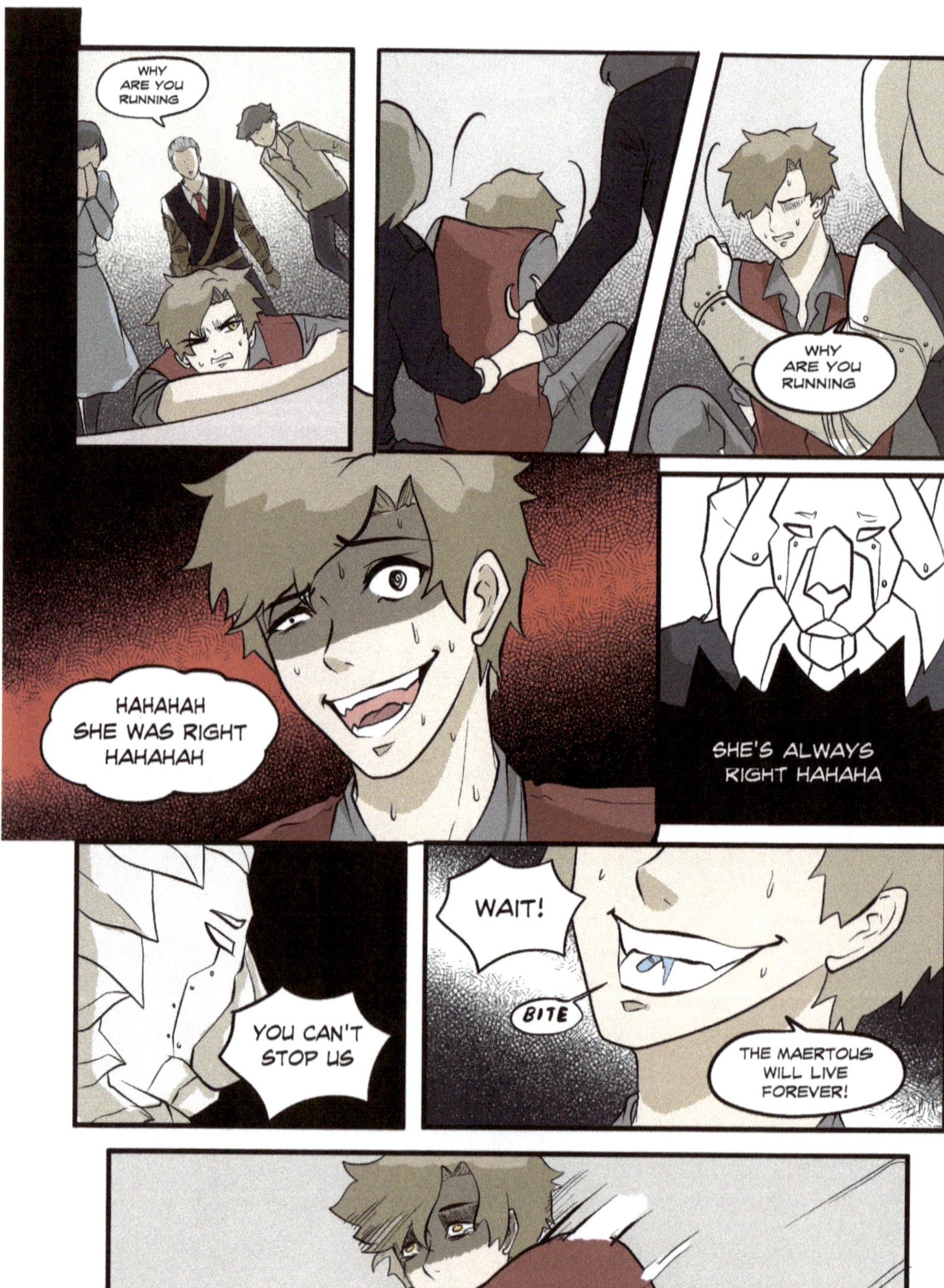

WHY ARE YOU RUNNING
WHY ARE YOU RUNNING
HAHAHAH SHE WAS RIGHT HAHAHAH
SHE'S ALWAYS RIGHT HAHAHA
YOU CAN'T STOP US
WAIT!
BITE
THE MAERTOUS WILL LIVE FOREVER!

WHO WAS HE REFERRING TO?
I... DONT KNOW
IS THE CHANCELLOR SAFE
YES, HE IS BEING ESCORTED TO THE CAPITAL BUILDING AS WE SPEAK
LET'S HEAD HOME

SHE'S ALWAYS RIGHT....

THE BANK IS BEING ROBBED!
HOW MANY AND WHEN!
I'VE BEEN WAITING FOR THIS

1 HOUR, UNSURE HOW MANY

YOU HAVE 10 MINUTES, AND THE BALLOON IS OFF

WAKE UP BOYS, ITS PARTY TIME
DO I HAVE TIME TO NAP?
LOOK SHARP, THE BANK IS JUST BELOW US
AND THERE THEY ARE
BANK

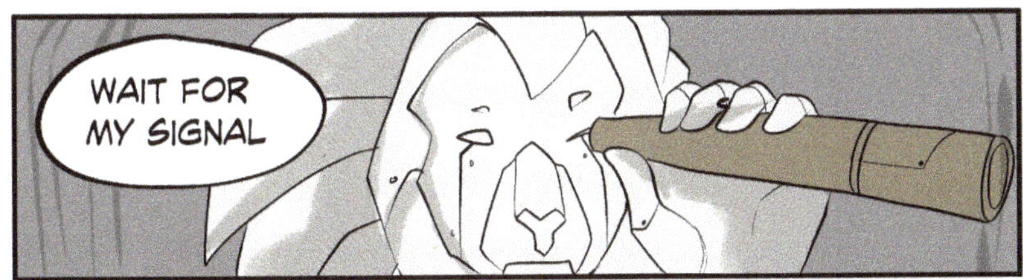

WAIT FOR MY SIGNAL

THE BAD GUYS ARE RIGHT THERE, LET JUST GO

Z

THEY HAVENT EVEN ENTERED YET DEMETRI, THEY HAVEN'T DONE ANYTHING WRONG

WHY ARE THERE PEOPLE LINING UP ALREADY?

WHY IS THE BANK HOSTING A JOB FAIR ANYWAY
THEY'RE NOT
YES, FINALLY!
ON THE GROUND!!!

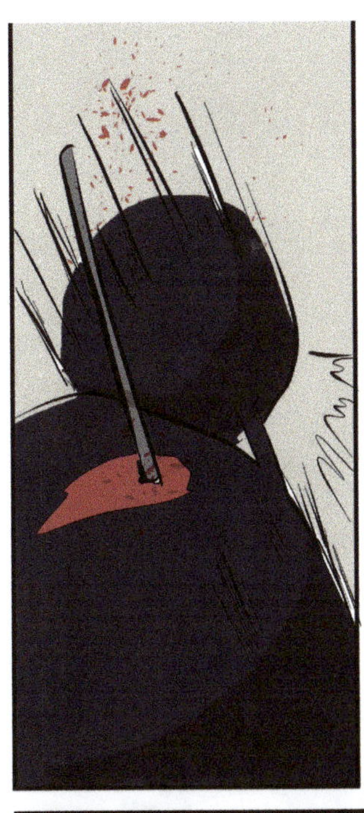

DONT MOVE
ANY FURTHER

THIS COULD HAVE
SOME.....
EXPLOSIVE
CONSEQUENCES

HEY
STOP MOVING

STOP!

BANGG

MURUM!
GRIME AND DIRT CAN ONLY BE CLEANSED
WITH FIRE AND BRIMSTONE
ALL HAIL THE MAERTOUS
BA-AMM

Aqueous!!
THIS IS BARNABAS AND THIS IS SYLAS, THEY'LL KEEP YOU SAFE

LET'S GO
HELLO CHANCELLOR

MARCOS, PLEASE EXPLAIN WHAT HAPPENED
CHANCELLOR THERE WASN'T..

IS YOUR NAME MARCOS?
NO
SO SIT DOWN AND SHUT UP

WHEN THE TIME AROSE, YOU ALL WERE SUPPOSED TO COME OUT OF HIDING AND DEFEND THIS REALM
5000 YEARS AGO YOU WERE CREATED FROM THE REMNANTS OF THE OLD GOD WHO SACRIFICED HIMSELF TO DEFEAT ELIGOS AND HIS LEGIONS
200 PEOPLE DIED TODAY

THERE HAS BEEN MORE BLOODSHED SINCE MY ELECTION LAST YEAR, THAN SINCE YOU ALL WERE CREATED

FIX IT, OR I WILL

WHAT WERE YOU DEFENDING

SH SH IT'S OKAY GO BACK TO SLEEP

THANK YOU FOR DOING THIS

WHEN ELIGOS WAS HERE..

HIS SOLDIERS WERE CREATED KNIGHTS FROM THE REALM OF GEHENNA

HE ENLIGHTENED ME, HE SHOWED ME HOW THEY WERE MADE
SHORTLY YOU WILL BECOME AN IBLIS

ALL HAIL THE MAERTOUS, AND LONG LIVE ELIGOS

HAHAHAHA

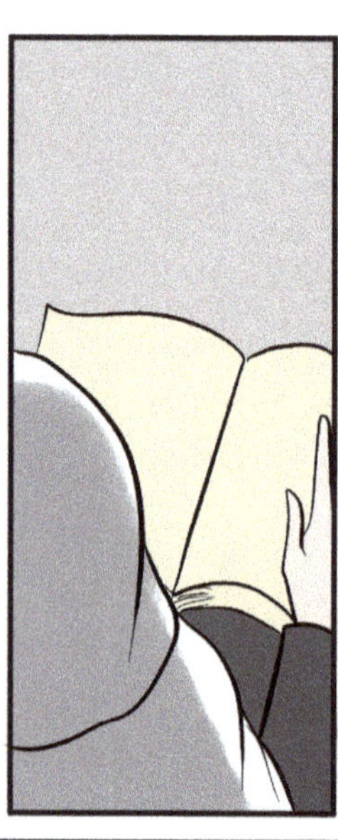

TH... THAT'S NOT POSSIBLE

WHAT IS IT KLAUS?

IBLIS

WHAT

THERE'S AN IBLIS IN ATLAS PARK

BUT HE'S DIFFERENT

HE'S STILL ALIVE

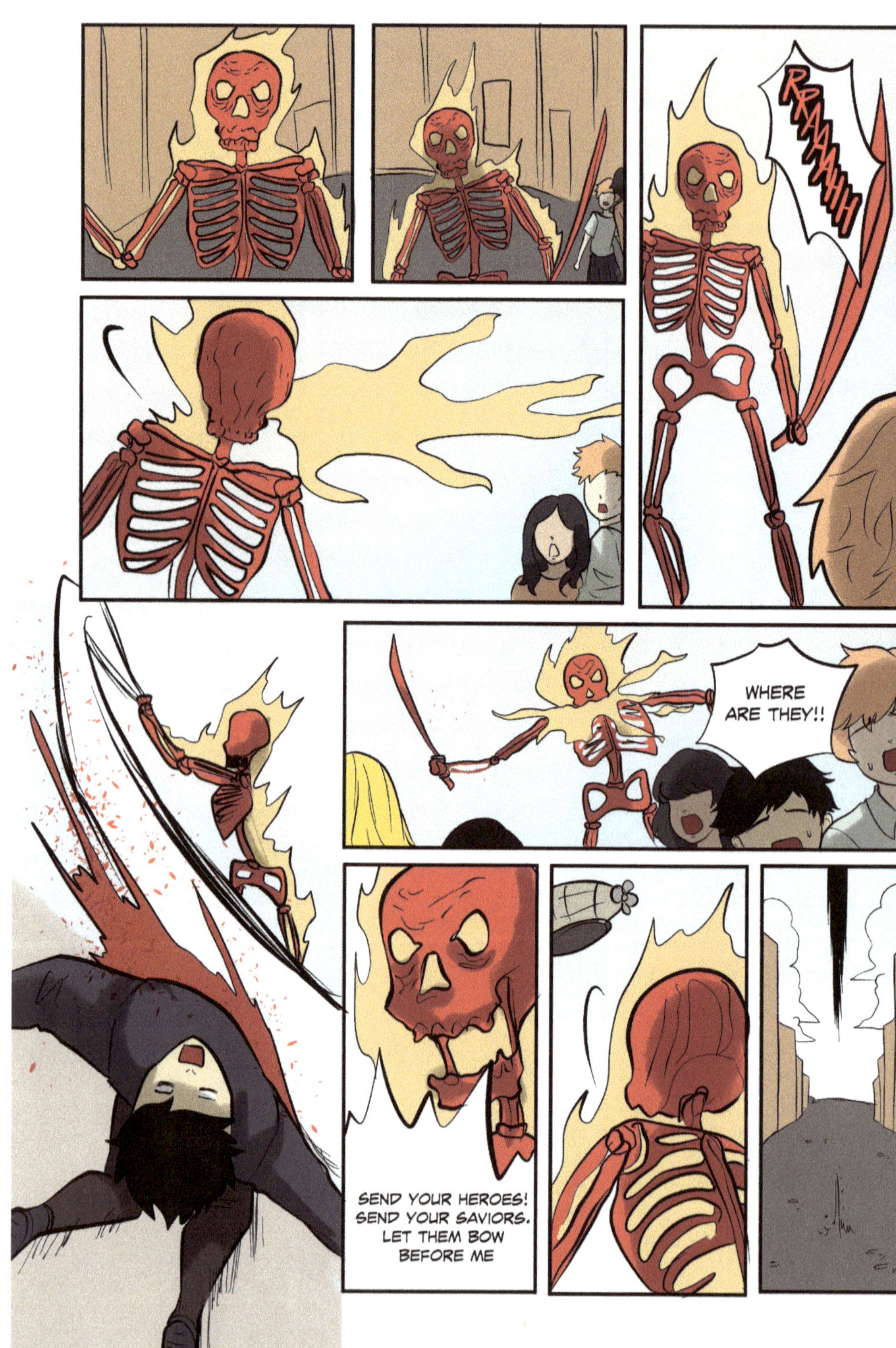

RRAAAHH
WHERE ARE THEY!!
SEND YOUR HEROES!
SEND YOUR SAVIORS.
LET THEM BOW
BEFORE ME

Ruzgar!

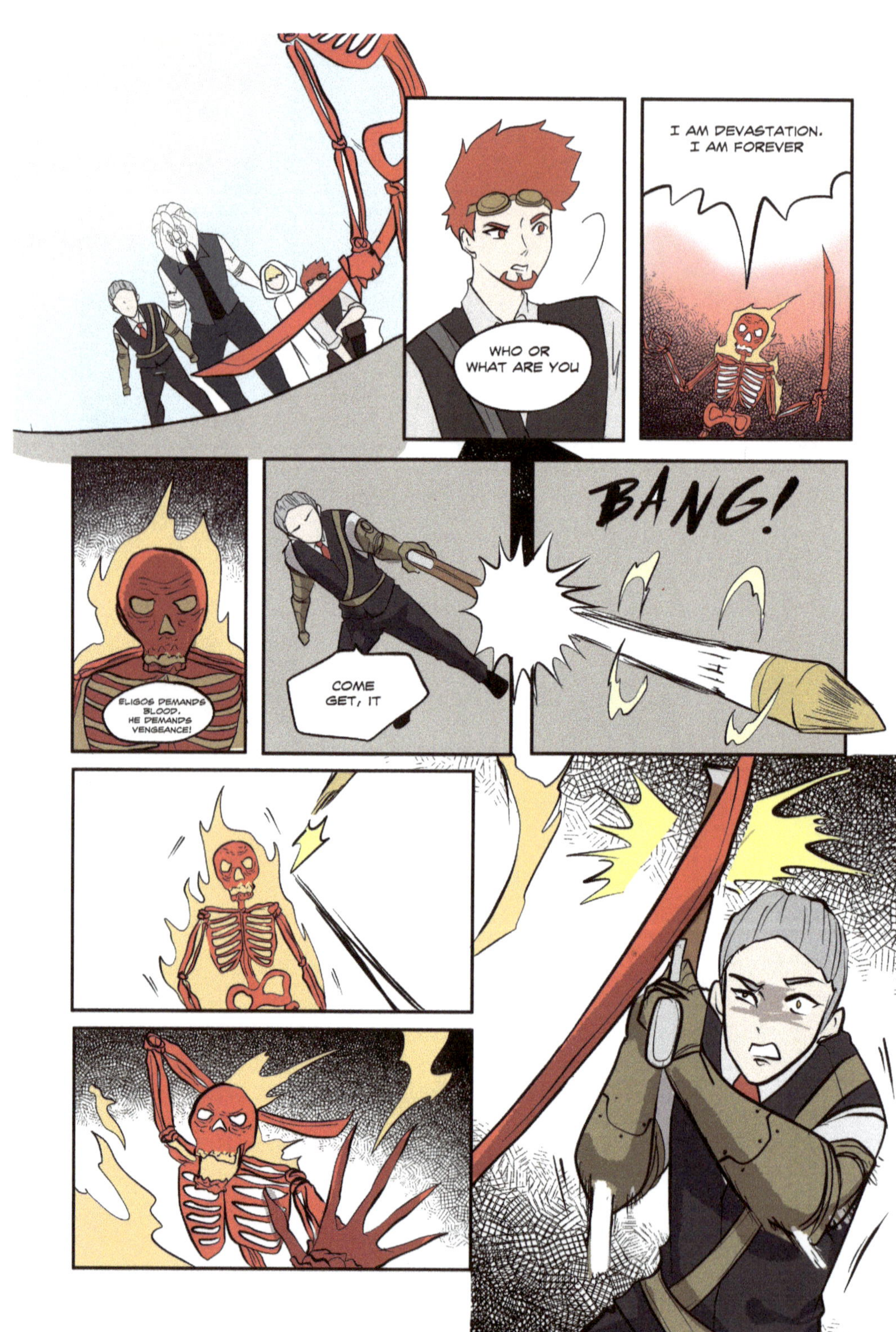
WHO OR WHAT ARE YOU
I AM DEVASTATION. I AM FOREVER
ELIGOS DEMANDS BLOOD. HE DEMANDS VENGEANCE!
COME GET, IT
BANG!

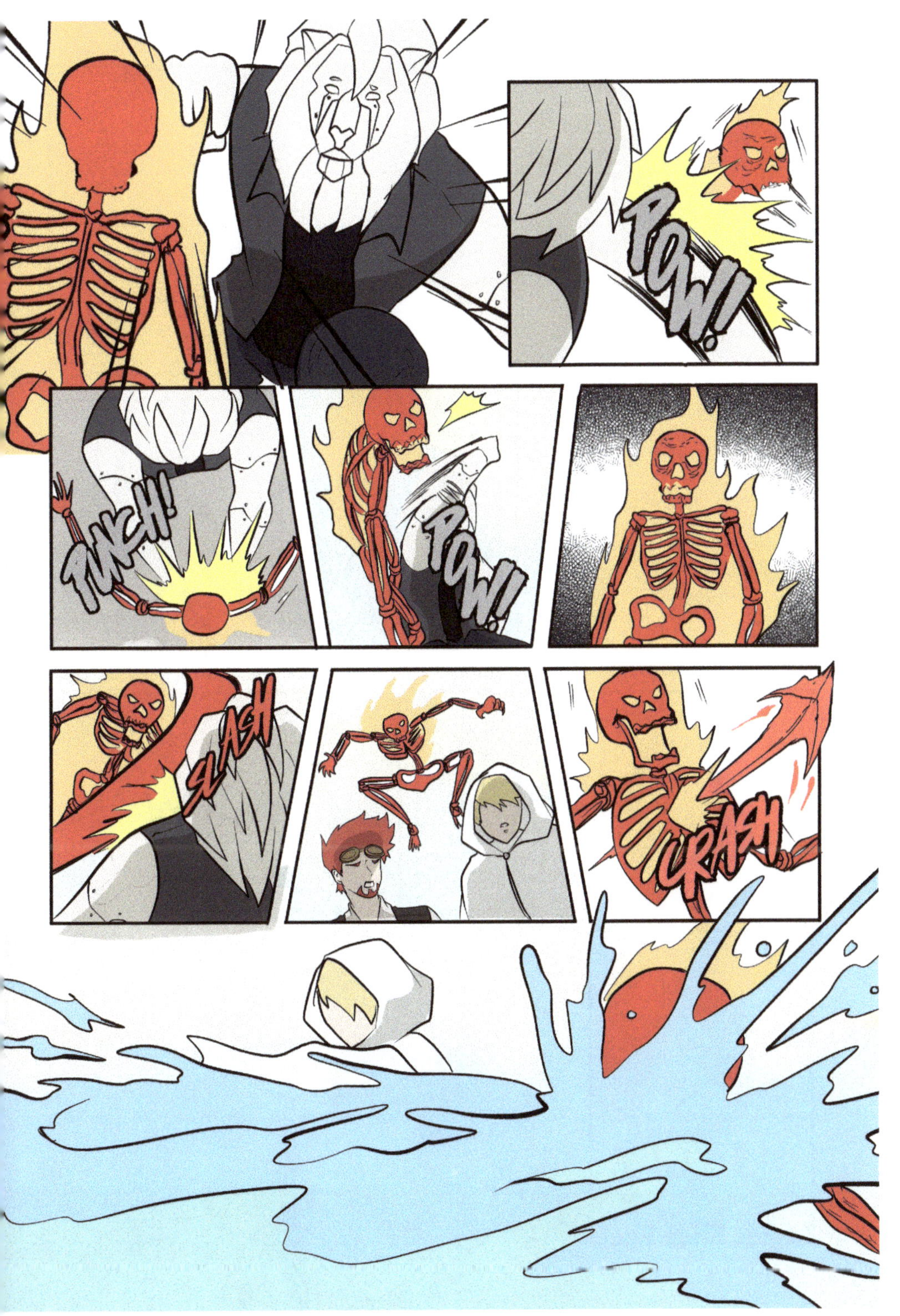
POW!
PUNCH!
POW!
SLASH
CRASH

CRACK
CRACK
BANG
!
FWOOOO

DO IT

Omnipotentia Creatoris

Michaelis...

Pugnare me Daemonia!

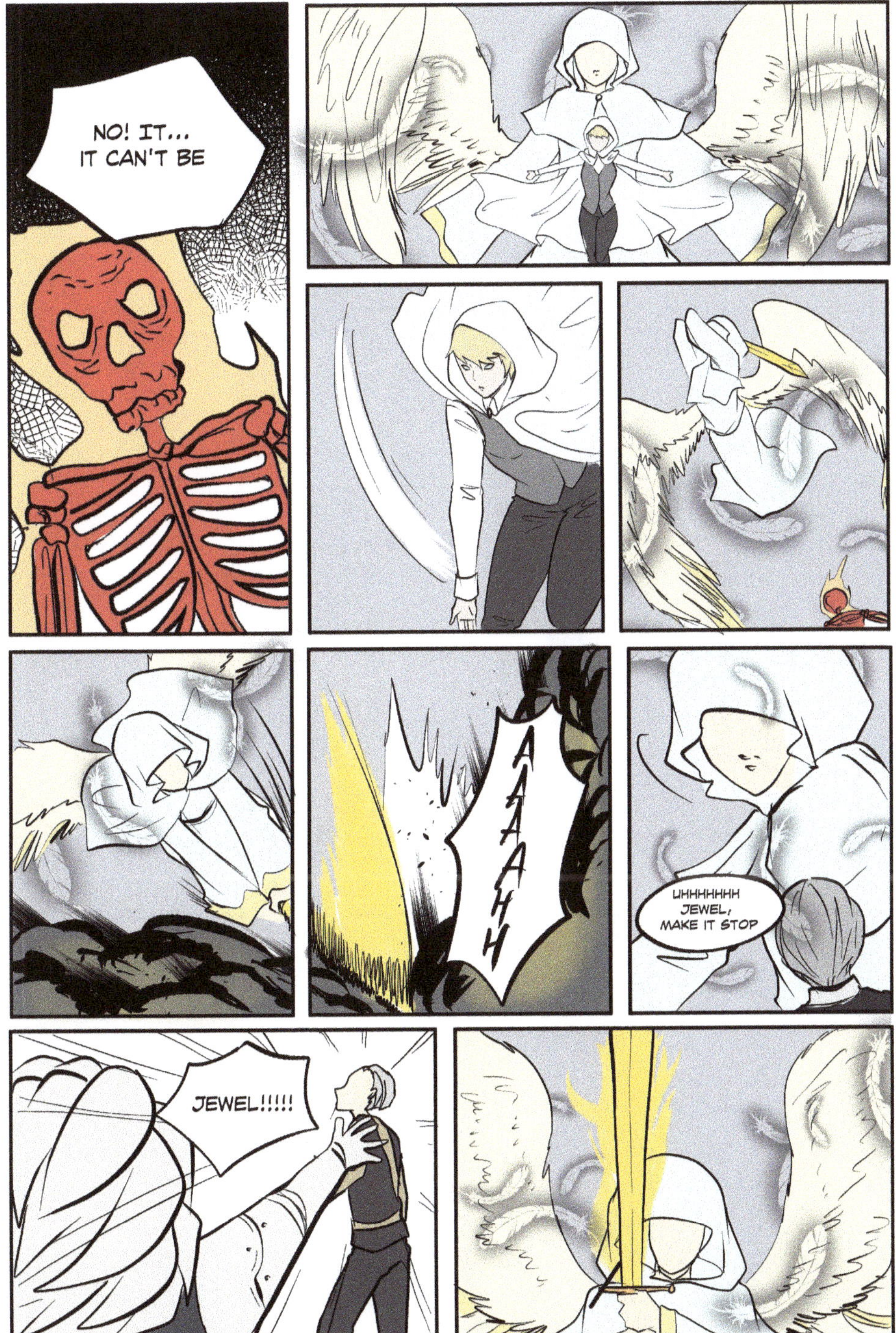

NO! IT...
IT CAN'T BE
AAAAHH
UHHHHHHH
JEWEL,
MAKE IT STOP
JEWEL!!!!!

Cease!

KLAUS RIDE WITH HER. DEMETRI AND I HAVE TO MEET WITH THE CHANCELLOR

HE'S BEEN EXPECTING YOU

CAN THEY ACTUALLY SUMMON HIM

NO, THAT WAS JUST AN IBLIS. BUT SOMEHOW DIFFERENT

WHAT DO YOU MEAN, DIFFERENT?
WE BELIEVE HE WAS SENTIENT

PRE-EXISTING

YOU MEAN
CREATED YES

THAT MEANS HE IS STRONGER THAN BEFORE

WHY DO WE HAVE TO GO TO THIS DUMB PRESS CONFERENCE

IT'S NOT DUMB AND WON'T EVEN BE SHOWN
WE ARE JUST THERE TO DETER ANY BAD GUYS
WHAT DOES THAT EVEN MEAN

SO WE GET TO PLAY BODYGUARD.
Yippie

YOU KNOW WE WOULDN'T BE HERE IF THE CHANCELLOR WASN'T CONCERNED ABOUT SOMETHING

I DIDN'T HAVE A VISION, IT MIGHT JUST BE NERVES

WELL WE'RE HERE NOW, LET'S MAKE THE BEST OF IT

HEY GUYS! THANKS FOR COMING!
YOU SEEM EXCITED
SHAKE
YES OF COURSE! TODAY IS THE DAY I REVEAL MY BIG PLAN

LADIES AND GENTLEMEN! I AM SO EXCITED TO ANNOUNCE THE NEXT STEP IN OUR INITIATIVE TO IMPROVE THE LIVES OF OUR LESS FORTUNATE BROTHERS AND SISTERS!

I VOWED,
I PROMISED,
I SWORE, TO NEVER
ALLOW THAT TO HAPPEN
TO ANYONE ELSE

GROWING UP,
I WAS POOR AND
FELT ABANDONED.
I WENT TO BED SCARED
AND HUNGRY MORE
NIGHTS THAN I CAN COUNT
SO TODAY WE START
A NEW INITIATIVE TO
INCREASE THE LIVELIHOOD
OF ALL HERE
IN ATLAS PARK

WE WILL
INCREASE
SPENDING IN ALL FIELDS
TO PROVIDE JOBS,
SHELTER AND FOOD
FOR THOSE
LESS FORTUNATE

. . . . .

LET US RID POVERTY ONCE AND FOR ALL

I'M NOT SURE WHERE HE WENT

IT'S REALLY NOT THAT BIG IF A DEAL, HE PROBABLY WANTED TO GET A BETTER VIEW

HOW?

WHAT NOW MARCOS

DEMETRI, GO GET THE KNIFE

SON THAT WAS QUITE DANGEROUS
NOT TO MENTION YOU USED YOUR POWER IN FRONT OF HUNDREDS OR EVEN THOUSANDS
MY LOVE, NO ONE EVEN NOTICED

BESIDES DID YOU SEE HOW EXCITED EVERYONE IS? THEY'RE ON OUR SIDE!

YES, THE PLAN IS WORKING OUT PERFECTLY.

THERE WILL BE NO MORE POOR PEOPLE IN ATLAS PARK

DEMETRI

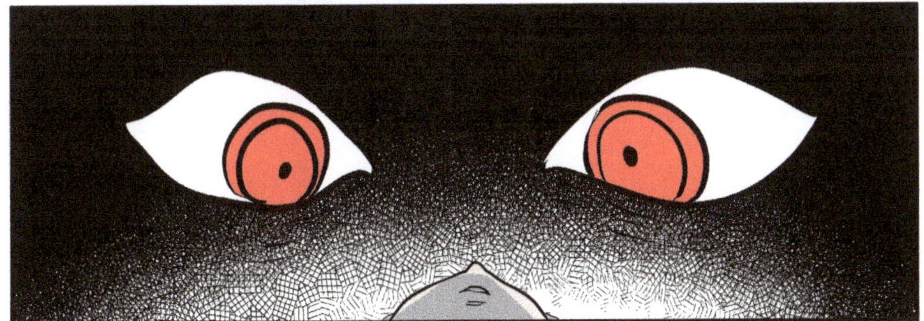

WHO'S THERE?

WHAT THE..

WHAT ARE YOU

DEMETRI, I DON'T SEE ANYTHING OUT OF THE ORDINARY
IT'S JUST A BLADE
KLAUS! I SWEAR IT SPOKE TO ME!
HE WILL NEVER BELIEVE YOU
YOU CAN'T HEAR THIS !?
WHAT DO YOU MEAN DEMETRI? ARE YOU OKAY??
GIVE ME HIS HEART. LIFE IS WASTED ON HUMANS. YOU ARE ALL A DISEASE

NO.
I'LL DO ANYTHING,
BUT I WON'T
HURT MY FRIENDS

ARE THEY EVEN
YOUR FRIENDS?

LET'S
FIND OUT

I'M SORRY

NO,
I'M SORRY

WHAT JUST
HAPPENED

DEMETRI IS IN
A FIGHT,
ONE WE
CAN'T HELP

I THOUGHT I'VE SEEN THAT BLADE BEFORE

IT'S THE HARBINGER
PRINCIPA, ELIGOS' SACRIFICIAL BLADE

IT'S THE STRAW, ATTACHED DIRECTLY TO THE MOUTH OF DESTRUCTION

DEMETRI WILL NEED OUR HELP

SO WHAT DO WE DO

ME AND JEWEL NEED TO WARN THE CHANCELLOR. YOU NEED TO CALL FOR AIDE
AIDE?
DO YOU REMEMBER ENOCH?

WAIT, WOAH WOAH

YOU KNOW WE WILL NEED HIS HELP TO DEFEAT THIS THING

B B BUT.. HE'S AN OLD GOD, FULL OF HATE AND ANGER

EXACTLY

MARCOS. JEWEL.
WHAT ARE YOU
GUYS DOING HERE?

SIR,
THE MAERTOUS.
THEY'RE...

I KNEW IT
LOOKED FAMILIAR.
SHE WAS RIGHT

WHAT DOES
THAT MEAN?
WHO IS SHE!?

M M MY MOTHER.
SHE SAID
THE BLADE WAS
FROM ELIGOS

PEOPLE THINK I'VE ALWAYS HAD A LIFE OF LUXURY. THEY THINK I COME OUT OF NO WHERE. LIKE A POOF OF MAGIC AND I APPEAR
THE MAERTOUS WANT ME DEAD BECAUSE THE PEOPLE LOOK TO ME AS A SAVIOR. A CLEANSER OF POVERTY. A LIBERATOR
BUT I'VE WORKED MY FINGERS TO THE BONE! GROWING AND LEARNING. SLOWLY UNDERSTANDING THE POLITICS OF GOVERNING PEOPLE HERE IN ATLAS PARK.
I AM JUST THE BEGINNING. OTHERS WILL COME BETTER THAN I AM. WE WILL CLEANSE THIS WORLD

SO DUMB. THEY HAVE ME. GOING BY MYSELF. TO CONVINCE A GUY. THAT HATES US. TO FIGHT ALONG SIDE US!
NO. NO WAY

SNAP
IGNIS
FAX!

SHE SEES THINGS, AND SHE IS ALWAYS RIGHT

FSS
SSH

SHE MUST BE AS BLIND AS I AM

P....P..PLEASE DON'T HURT ME

WHY WOULD I HURT YOU?

YOU DON'T HATE US?

THE 4 OF YOU WERE MADE FROM THE SPIRIT OF MY FRIEND, GESU.

THE PASSION IGNITING INSIDE BURNS IN A DIFFERENT COLOR FOR YOU THAN ELIGOS

WHY WON'T YOU SPEAK TO ME!
FINE, YOU DON'T WANT ME? I DEFINITELY DON'T WANT YOU!
HEY
YA KNOW, DEMETRI, LADY EVELYN TOLD US YOU'D BE HERE
ALL ALONE. CONFUSED. SHE EVEN USED THE WORD DERANGED
SO IN ESSENCE, WE'RE JUST PUTTING DOWN A RABID DOG. UNHINGED, AFRAID AND BACKED INTO A CORNER
THIS IS MERCY

MORE!

LADY EVELYN! THE CHAMBER IS FILLING!
ELIGOS

WHY DID WE BELIEVE YOU HATED US?
WHEN GESU SACRIFICED HIMSELF, I WAS OVERCOME WITH ANGER AND SHAME THAT I WAS USELESS IN THE FIGHT AGAINST ELIGOS. I FLED
AND WHERE DID YOU AND GESU AND ELIGOS COME FROM

HE CREATED EVERYTHING THAT YOU KNOW IN EXISTENCE. AND EVEN MORE THAT YOU DON'T
BEFORE THE CREATION OF THIS PHYSICAL DIMENSION, THERE WAS ONE BEING. THE SOUL CREATOR
LASTLY, HE CREATED HUMANITY. HIS FAVORITE CREATION. HIS BELOVED
HE CREATED AN ORDER OF 200 BEINGS, THE WATCHERS, TO PROTECT HUMANITY. YOUR KIND REFERRED TO US AS "OLD GODS"
HE BECAME FUELED BY JEALOUSY AND STARTED SLAUGHTERING THE THINGS HE WAS CREATED TO PROTECT
SAMJAZA WAS THE STRONGEST OF ALL OF US. HE WAS OUR LEADER. HE HAD UNIMAGINABLE POWER

ELIGOS, GESU AND MYSELF CONFRONTED SAMJAZA
AND WHEN WE HAD ALMOST SLAIN OUR ADVERSARY, ELIGOS TURNED ON US
SAMJAZA ESCAPED THAT FATEFUL DAY. WE HAD FOUGHT ELIGOS FOR CENTURIES AFTER THAT

ON THIS ONE PARTICULAR DAY, ELIGOS WAS STRONGER THAN NORMAL. GESU AND I COULD NOT DO ANYTHING TO HIM.
HE WOUNDED ME, RIPPING OFF MY WINGS. SO I FLED. LEAVING GESU ALONE

THE EXPLOSION COULD BE SEEN FOR GALAXIES. GESU SACRIFICED HIMSELF THAT DAY. THE SOUL CREATOR, MOVED BY GESU'S COMPASSION CREATED THE 4 OF YOU OUT OF HIS REMAINS SPIRIT

I NEVER HATED YOU ALL. I LOVE YOU ALL. YOU ARE THE ESSENCE OF MY CLOSEST FRIEND

MARCOS IS EXPECTING US BACK ANYTIME NOW KLAUS

ENOCH!

YOU SHALL BOW BEFORE NO ONE!

YOU HAVE THE SAME VALOR AND HONOR AS GESU

YOU LOOK A LITTLE SCRATCHED UP KLAUS! WHAT HAPPENED?

JUST HANDLED A GROUP OF MAERTOUS BY MYSELF! NO PROBLEM

I AM UNEASY ABOUT THE CHANCELLOR. HE HAS ALL OF THESE PLANS, BUT IT SEEMS ALL TO FARFETCHED

WHY IS THAT?

HE WANTS TO HAVE A HUGE FEAST FOR ALL OF THE POOR TOWNSFOLK TOMORROW!
THATS AMAZING! WHATS WRONG WITH THAT?

AFTER THE BANK INCIDENT, IT DOESN'T SEEM WISE TO HAVE A HUGE GATHERING AGAIN

YOUR EYES ARE NOT TRICKING YOU

HOW CAN WE FREE HIM?

THE BLADE PROVIDES FUEL FOR THE BLOOD LUST OF ELIGOS, BUT IT'S NOT HIS BLADE
WHAT?

IT BELONGS TO SAMJAZA

SAMJAZA USED IT TO CORRUPT THE MIND OF ELIGOS. AND NOW, UNFORTUNATELY, DEMETRI

HIS POWER GROWS AND SHRINKS BASED OFF OF THE BLOOD LUST OF THE WIELDER
SO IT'S UP TO DEMETRI TO RESIST IT?
AND THEN IT CAN BE BROKEN COMPLETELY

WHOM DO YOU SERVE?
I..
BOOM
GO! GO! GO!

WHERE ARE YOU OFF TO SO FAST?

WHO'S THERE?
STEP OUT OF THE SHADOW COWARD!

AIN'T YOU ON OUR SIDE NOW?

HIT HIS KNEE

BANG

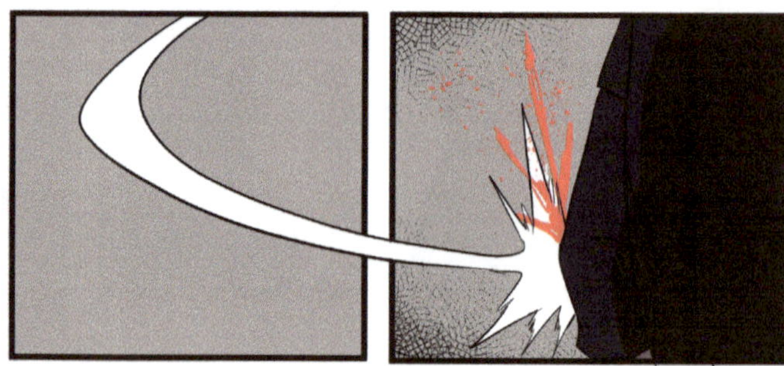

NOT
EXACTLY

BANG

WHOM DO YOU SERVE?

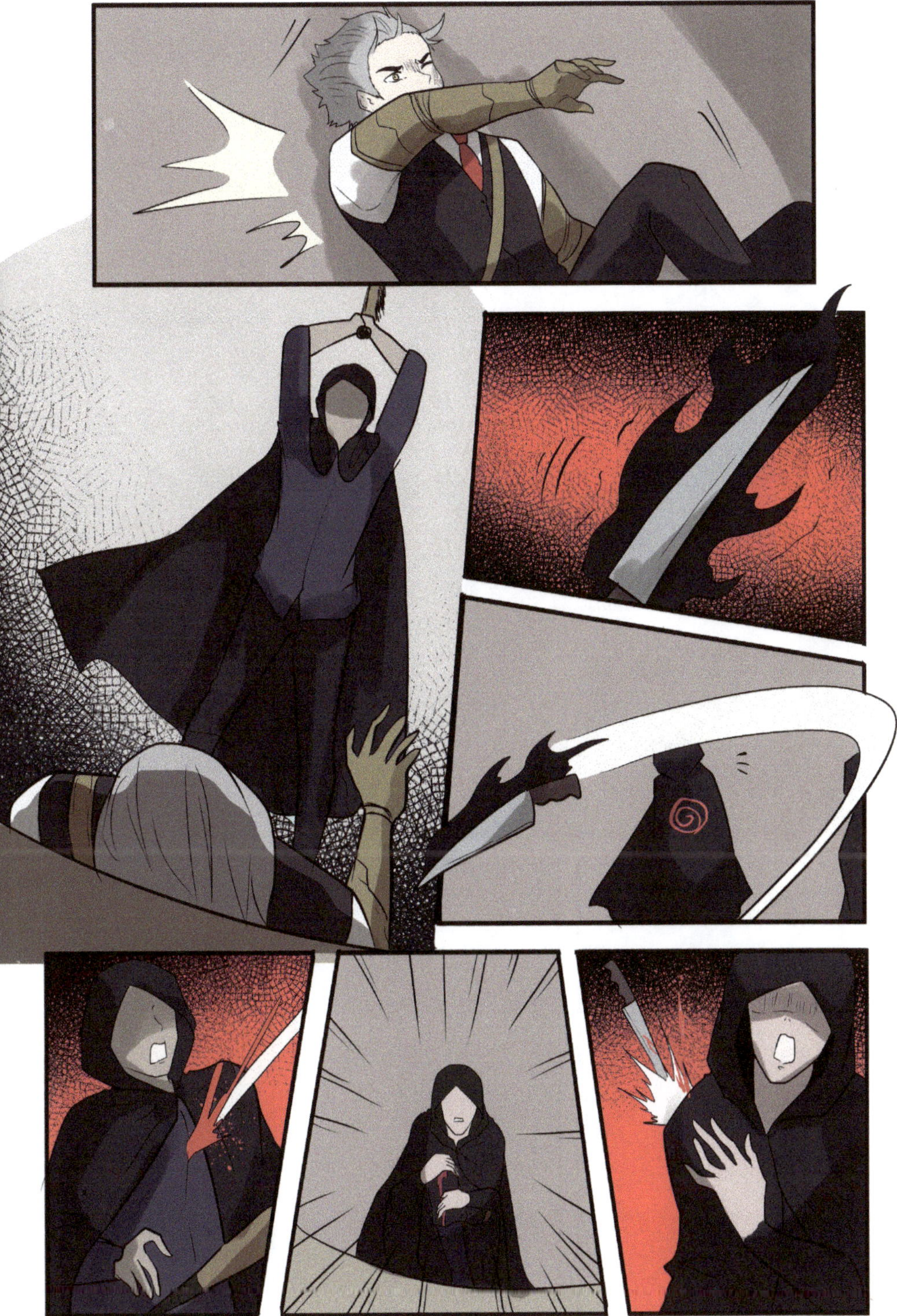

THIS IS THE SECOND TIME I'VE SAVED YOU

YOU SERVE ME NOW! WE HAVE A DINNER TO ATTEND.

WHAT ARE YOU RUNNING FROM, DEMETRI?

I... I DON'T KNOW, BUT I CAN'T STOP

HAVE YOU FOUND MASTER? IS HE SAFE?
LET'S GO INSIDE
HE BLAMES HIMSELF FOR WHAT IS HAPPENING TO DEMETRI

HISTORY WILL BE MADE TODAY

FOR MY SAFETY AND THE SAFETY OF EVERYONE HERE, I WILL NOT STAY LONG
AS EXPECTED, SIR
GOOD

ANY NEWS OF DEMETRI?
NONE SIR

LET THEM IN

BROTHERS AND SISTERS!

I STAND IN UNISON WITH YOU. YOU ARE NOT ABANDONED. YOU ARE NOT FORGOTTEN

THIS IS SYMBOLIC OF THE PROSPERITY THAT WILL COME TO ALL IN ATLAS PARK

WE FEAST TODAY AS FAMILY. WE EAT AS ROYALTY

DON'T WORRY SIR. WE WILL STAY AND MAKE SURE EVERYTHING GOES SMOOTHLY
GOOD

I'M SURE YOU'VE SEEN THIS COMING, KLAUS
BUT DID YOU EXPECT THIS?, KLAUS

BAM

BAM

BAM

BAM

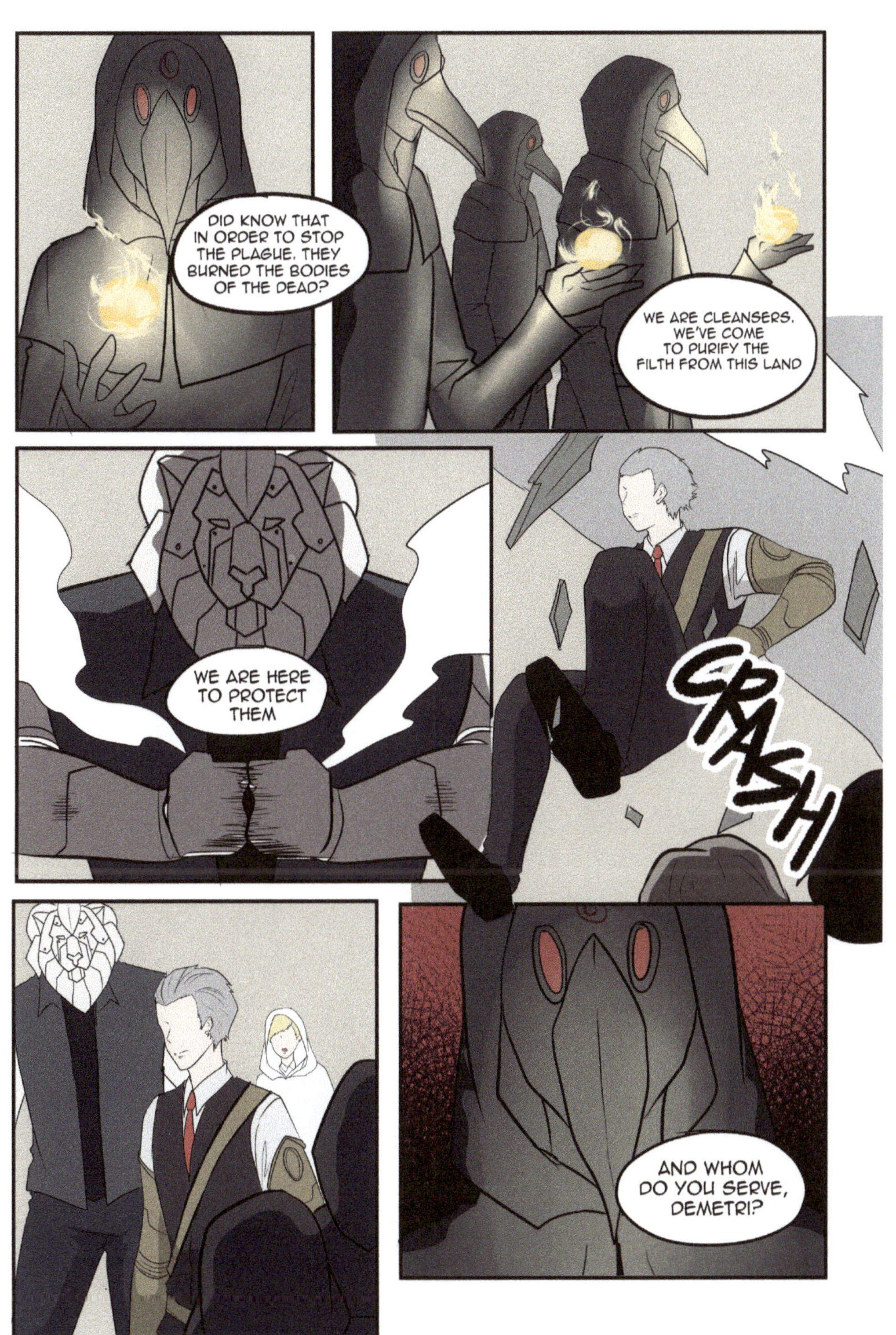

DID KNOW THAT IN ORDER TO STOP THE PLAGUE, THEY BURNED THE BODIES OF THE DEAD?
WE ARE CLEANSERS. WE'VE COME TO PURIFY THE FILTH FROM THIS LAND
WE ARE HERE TO PROTECT THEM
CRASH
AND WHOM DO YOU SERVE, DEMETRI?

!

!

LAPIS!

POW

SHINK
ALL HAIL THE MAERTOUS AND LONG LIVE ELIGOS

HA
HA
HA
HA
LONG LIVE ELIGOS

ELIGOS IS NEARING HIS FULL POWER ONCE AGAIN

WHEN I CREATED THE IBLIS, I WAS JUST TESTING THE STRENGTH OF THESE "NEW GODS"

I WAS HOPING PRINCIPA, ELIMINATING DEMETRI, WOULD HAVE BEEN ENOUGH, BUT FLIGHT TEAM IS STRONG

MOTHER, LADY EVELYN. MY LOVE, LILITH. AND MY BEAUTIFUL DAUGHTER, LUCY...

WE HAVE TO KILL FLIGHT TEAM

BOOMM
DEMETRI PLEASE.
BROTHER....
HELP US
GET KLAUS HOME
AT THE VERY LEAST

CAN YOU FIGHT?

AAAAH

THIS FLAME SHOULD BE ENOUGH TO CAUTERIZE THE WOUND I HOPE
WATCH OUT!
YOU CAN BEAT HIM JEWEL. JUST DON'T GO ANGEL FORM. BEAT HIM AS YOU ARE. YOU CAN DO IT

AAHH!
WITH YOU AND THE REST OF FLIGHT TEAM FALLING, ELIGOS WILL RULE ATLAS PARK WITH AN IRON FIST
POW

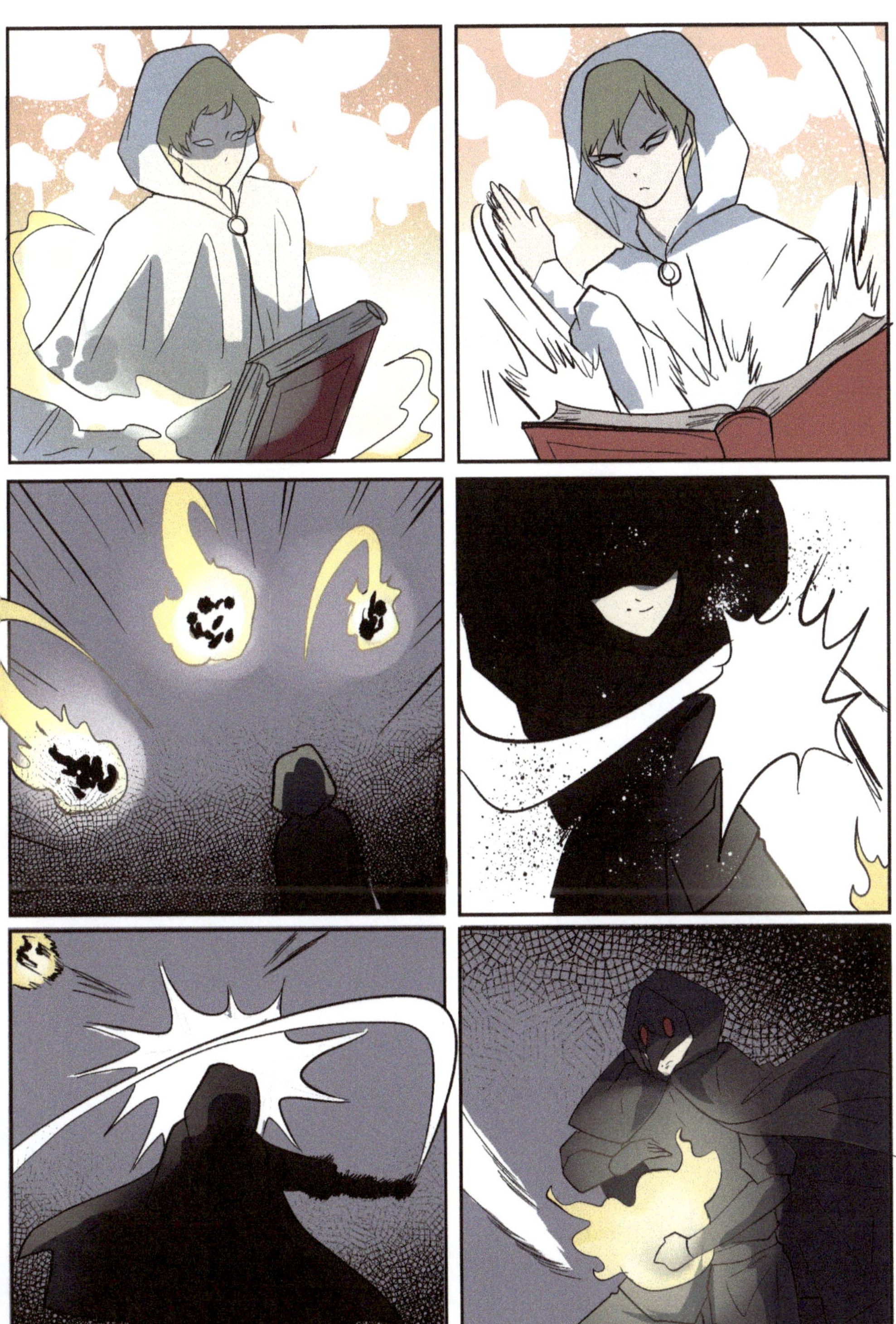

AAHHH
AAHHH
ESH
ELOAH

YOU DIDN'T FAIL US, JEWEL! YOU DIDN'T FAIL DEMETRI OR THE PEOPLE HERE!

HA HA HA YOU WERE DESTINED TO DIE HERE

YOU'VE SAVED SO MANY ALREADY!
AND IF YOU BEAT HIM HERE AND NOW, YOU CAN SAVE SO MANY MORE

SNKKTT

DO IT NOW JEWEL!

ЛЛЛЛЛ

AHHH

THIS IS IT DEMETRI,
WE CAN FINALLY
END IT.
RIGHT NOW

MASTER!
MASTER DON'T!

LADY EVELYN WAS RIGHT AGAIN DEMETRI. SHE SAID THIS WOULD HAPPEN. SHE ALSO SAID NOT TO LET YOU GO

BOW

BAM

WE CAN GET OUT OF HERE, BUT WE NEED TO WORK TOGETHER. IF YOU WANT TO RUN AWAY AGAIN. I WON'T STOP YOU

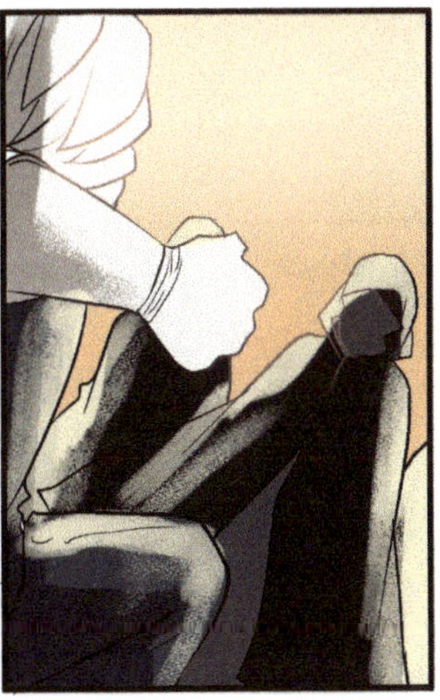

NOT THIS TIME
KAPOW!
DINK!
GET OFF OF HIM!
BANG!
MARCOS! MARCOS!

DEMETRI,
WHY WOULD YOU
EVER TURN YOUR BACK
IN BATTLE?
DON'T HURT
MY MASTER!
MASTER?
ARE YOU
OKAY?
BEEP
SYLAS!
GET OUT OF HERE
BEFORE YOU
GET HURT!
WE MISSED
YOU MASTER.
YOU AREN'T
THE SAME
BEEP
BEEP

BEEP
GET OFF OF ME!
BEEP
BEEP
NEVER FORGET ME, MASTER
BEEP
NO! SYLAS! WHAT ARE YOU DOING!? STOP!!!
BEEP
BEEP
DON'T FORGET ME

I I'M, DEMETRI, I'M...
NO! YOU DON'T GET TO BE SORRY MARCOS!
THIS. THIS RIGHT HERE IS ALL YOUR FAULT!
HE LIVES IN MY MIND. HE'S CONSTANTLY SPEAKING TO ME. ALWAYS! JUST WHISPERING TO ME ALL DAY!
....AND IT'S ALL YOUR FAULT

WHY DID YOU CHOOSE ME?
YOU ARE DOING THE RIGHT THING. CONTINUE TO DESTROY HIS MORALE. THEY WILL ALL BEND TO THE WILL OF ELIGOS
LOOK OUT OVER THE CITY, MY CHILD.......
.... AT THE END OF IT ALL, YOU WILL RULE
ALL YOU HAVE TO DO IS BOW TO ME
SO I ASK YOU AGAIN, WHOM DO YOU SERVE?

ELIGOS NEEDS BLOOD TO REGAIN HIS STRENGTH...
.. SO HERE HAVE SOME BLOOD. THAT'S WHAT YOU WANT ISN'T IT?"
ISN'T THAT WHAT YOU WANT?
ANSWER ME!
STAB

YOUR ONLY DESIRE IS DESTRUCTION. DESTRUCTION OF ME, ATLAS PARK, AND HUMANITY AS WHOLE
THIS FACADE OF GLORIOUS VICTORY AND CONQUEST WAS SOLELY FOR YOU
YOU KNEW FOR A WHILE I WAS NOT ON YOUR SIDE. YOUR LIES, DRENCHED IN A SWEET AROMA, ARE LACED WITH POTENT POISON
GO AHEAD! SPEAK TO ME! SAVE YOURSELF! YOU'RE THE ONLY THING YOU CARED FOR ANYWAY

EVERY NIGHT, YOU WILL STIR IN HORROR AS MY MEMORY WILL PLAGUE YOU
YOU'LL NEVER BE RID OF ME DEMETRI
YOUR REGRET WILL SWALLOW YOU ALIVE. ALL THE WHILE, YOU WILL BE HUNTED. A TRAITOR RIGHTFULLY MARKED FOR DEATH..
...THERE IS NO MERCY IN A WORLD RULED BY ELIGOS. YOU WILL DIE UNLESS YOU BOW TO ME!
WHOM DO YOU SERVE?

GESU!

WE ARE SAFE NOW, JEWEL. YOU CAN SIT
NO, MARCOS. KLAUS, ENOCH AND DEMETRI ARE BARELY ALIVE AND THERE ARE MAERTOUS EVERYWHERE
WE ARE NEARLY AT ENOCH'S HOME. WE CAN HIDE OUT FOR AWHILE

STAY HERE AND STAY LOW. I'M GOING TO CHECK THE AREA
EVEN WHILE YOU WERE STILL FAR OFF, DEAR BROTHER, GESU WAS RUNNING OUT TO GREET YOU

CRAACK
IT'S ALL CLEAR,
LET'S HURRY

POOR ENOCH.
HE WAS OUTCAST
AND MISCONCEIVED
FOR DECADES

HE REDEEMED
HIMSELF TODAY AS
A WATCHER,
A PROTECTOR
OF HUMANITY

WHAT DO
WE DO NEXT
MARCOS?
WE WAIT.
WE HAVE TO ASSUME
THE CHANCELLOR IS
INVOLVED IN
ALL OF THIS

REST UP JEWEL.
THERE'S
WAR COMING ....

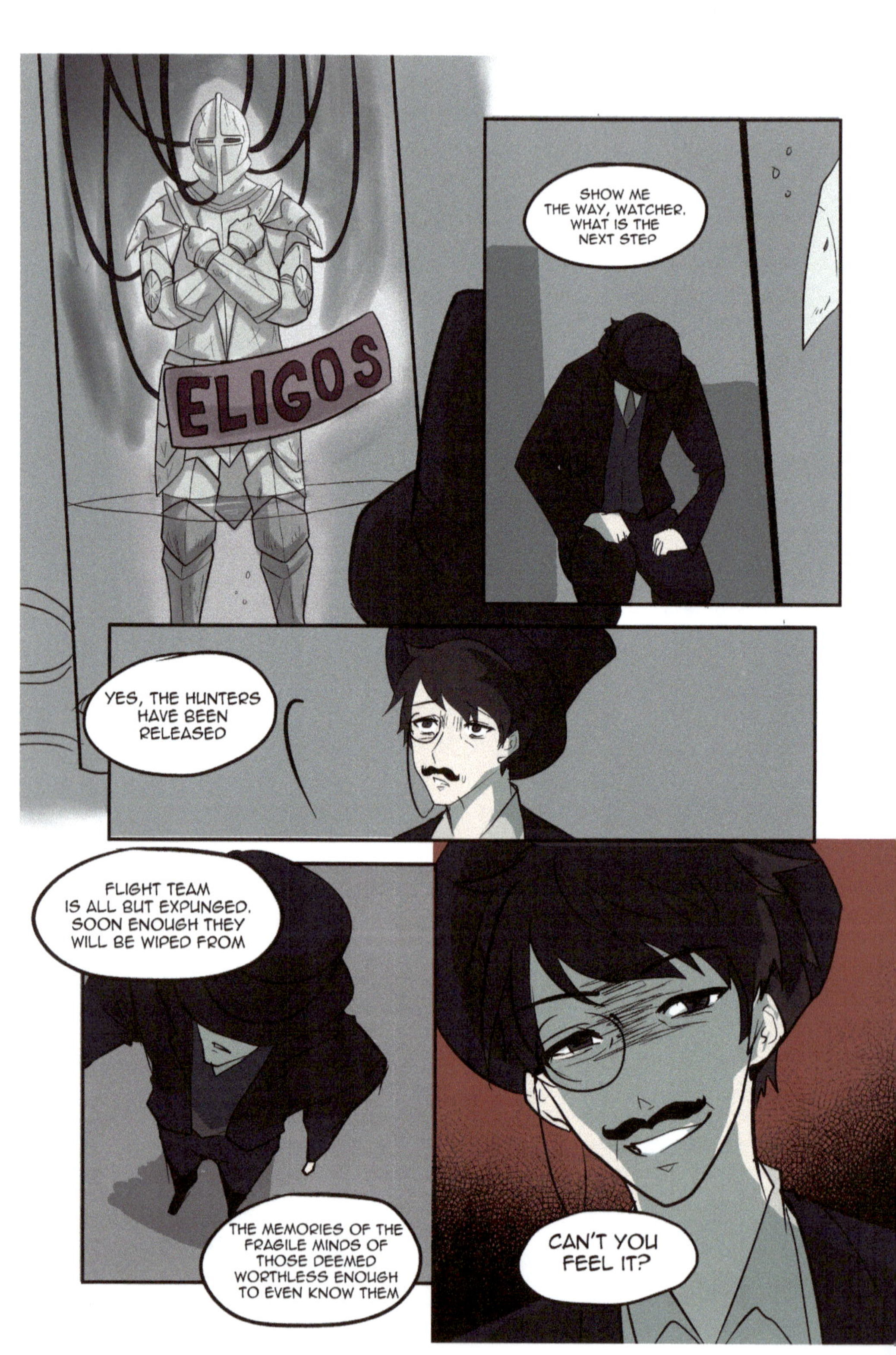
ELIGOS
SHOW ME THE WAY, WATCHER. WHAT IS THE NEXT STEP
YES, THE HUNTERS HAVE BEEN RELEASED
FLIGHT TEAM IS ALL BUT EXPUNGED. SOON ENOUGH THEY WILL BE WIPED FROM
THE MEMORIES OF THE FRAGILE MINDS OF THOSE DEEMED WORTHLESS ENOUGH TO EVEN KNOW THEM
CAN'T YOU FEEL IT?

AS EACH MOMENT PASSES, THEIR LIFE ESSENCE DWINDLES

THEY ARE GESU INCARNATE. THE SOLE PROTECTORS OF HUMANITY

CAN'T YOU FEEL THE BARRIER FADING, ELIGOS?

THIS WORLD IS NEARLY YOURS FOR THE TAKING

ELIGOS

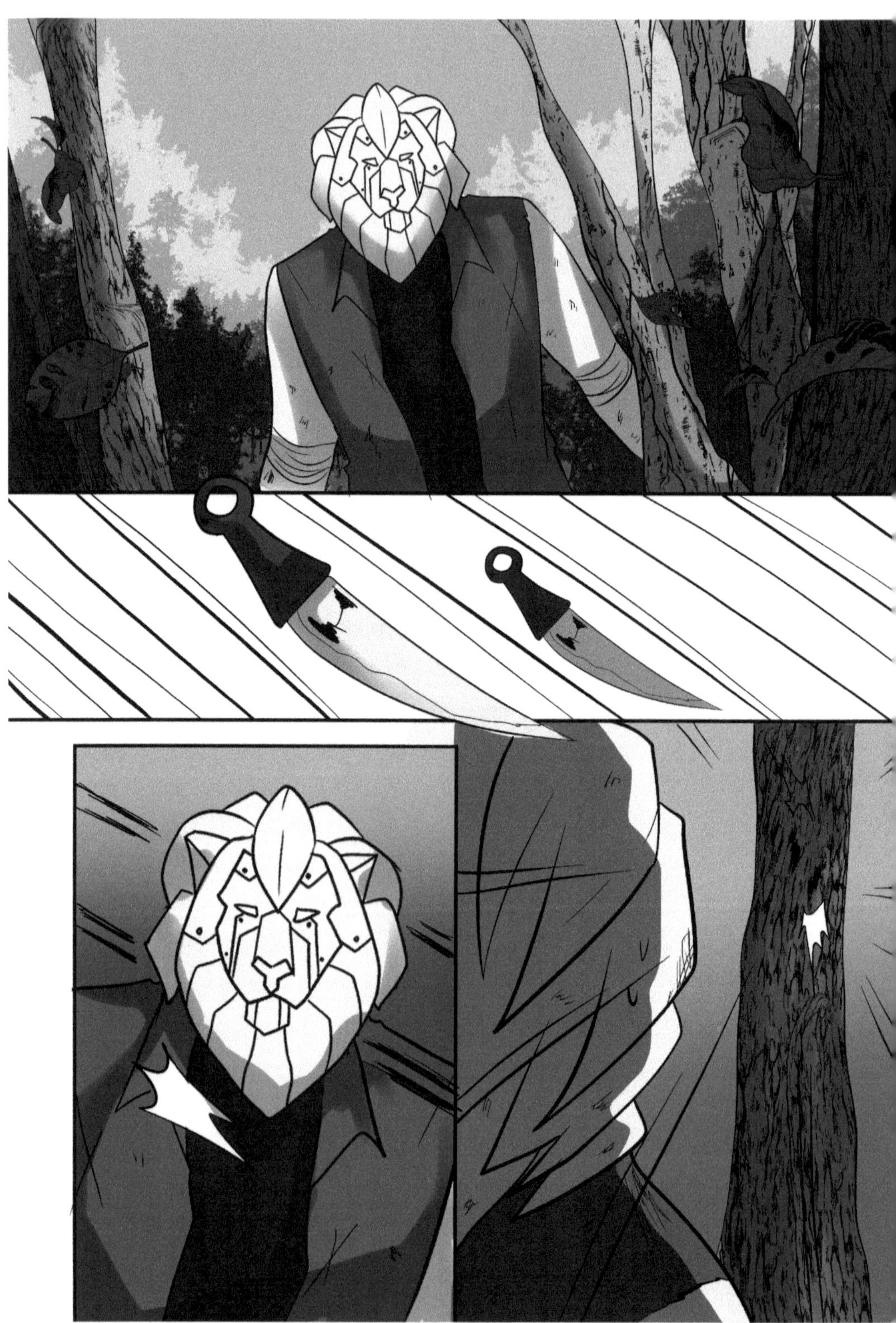

GRAMMA, SAID THE BIG LION WOULD BE READY TO PLAY
EXCEPT YOU LOOK LIKE TIRED, HUNGRY KITTY
COME HERE, KITTY KITTY

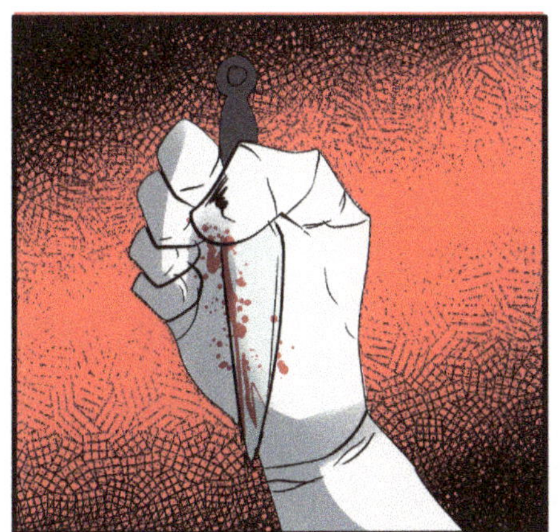
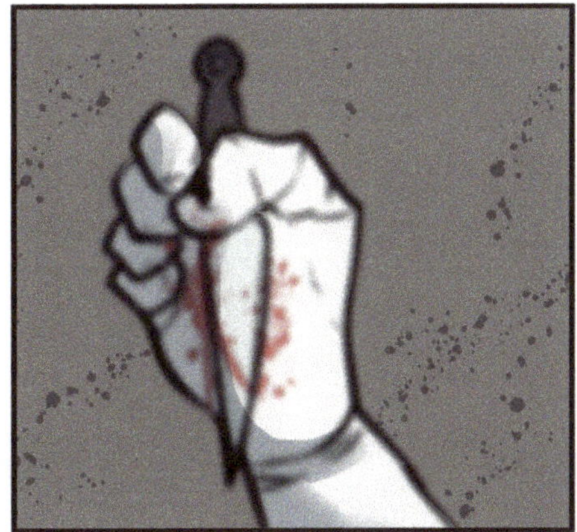

IS SOMETHING
WRONG
WITTLE KITTY?

THE
BLOOD OF ELIGOS
IS QUITE STRONG,
ISN'T IT?

I AM A SERVANT OF THIS WORLD
WIELDER OF THE GAUNTLETS OF KRINO
DELIVERER FROM DEVASTATION, AND PURGER OF THE PUTRID
LET THE WRATH OF THE INDIGNANT BURN
ROOAAARR

POW!
KITTY!
LET ME HEAR
THAT ROAR
AGAIN!

SCAREDY CAT!
COME BACK!
CRASH

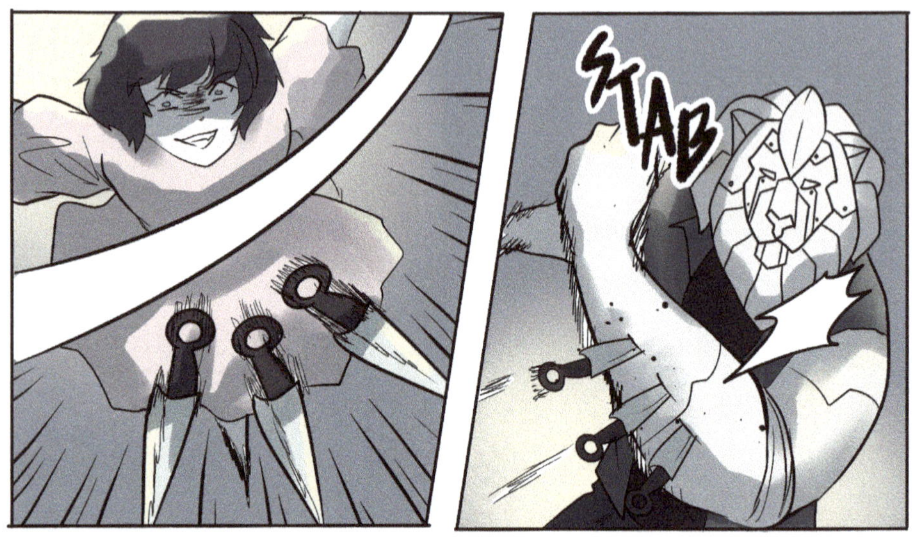

STAB

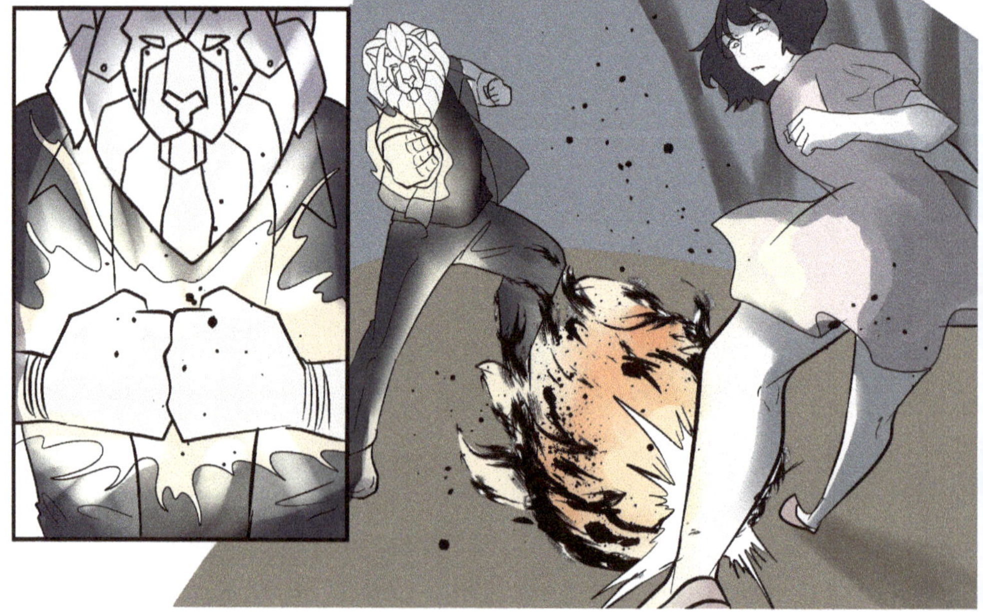

AHHHH
BAD KITTY!

PLEASE
STOP FIGHTING,
I DON'T MEAN TO
HURT YOU ANYMORE
THAN I HAVE
TO

HELLO, OLD FRIEND
I'M SURPRISED IT TOOK YOU THIS LONG
SIR! Y...Y...YOU'RE BEHIND THIS
RIGHT GUYS!
YES!

TAP

TAP

TAP

YOU PROBABLY ALREADY KNOW WHY YOU'RE HERE

GET IT OVER WITH

NOW, NOW. DON'T SPOIL THE MOMENT

ELIGOS HAS BEEN DREAMING OF THIS MOMENT FOR AGES

GESU... CAN YOU HEAR ME. GIVE ME STRENGTH

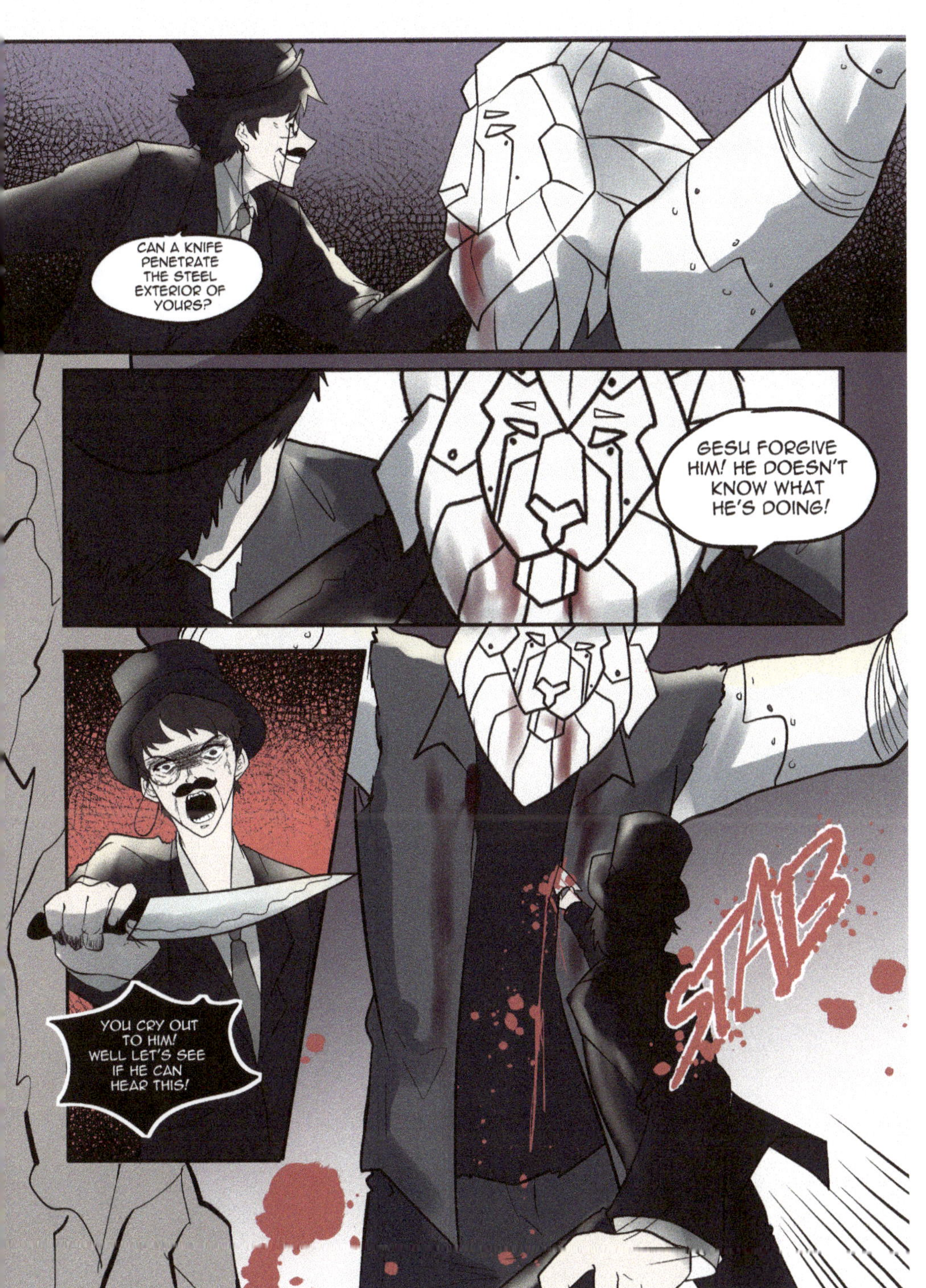

CAN A KNIFE PENETRATE THE STEEL EXTERIOR OF YOURS?
GESU FORGIVE HIM! HE DOESN'T KNOW WHAT HE'S DOING!
YOU CRY OUT TO HIM! WELL LET'S SEE IF HE CAN HEAR THIS!
STAB

GESU, PLEASE GIVE ME THE STRENGTH TO DO THIS
HA
HA
HA
HA
CAN HE HEAR YOU?
CRASH

GESU
IT IS FINISHED
CR
ASH

V1 studios

A passionate studio based out of long Island, New York, founded by Nicholas Garcia, the studio aims to bring high quality, story driven excitement across all mediums.

With a proven track record of video games, animation and now comic books, join us as we delve into "Flight Team". The brand-new epic from the studio delves into a team of 4 divinely blessed superheroes fighting to protect their city from demonic invasion.

If you like what you are reading, keep up with the studio on social media

@v1_studios_official

V1 CHURCH PODCAST
AVAILABLE ON ALL PLATFORMS

JOSEPH AND THE RAINBOW ROBE
AVAILABLE NOW ON IOS & GOOGLE PLAY
iOS   Google Play